YEARLING BOOKS/YOUNG YEARLINGS/YEARLING CLASSICS are designed especially to entertain and enlighten young people. Patricia Reilly Giff, consultant to this series, received the bachelor's degree from Marymount College. She holds the master's degree in history from St. John's University, and a Professional Diploma in Reading from Hofstra University. She was a teacher and reading consultant for many years, and is the author of numerous books for young readers.

For a complete listing of all Yearling titles, write to
Dell Readers Service, P.O. Box 1045,
South Holland, IL 60473.

The Old Tree Stories

Foolish
Miss Crow

PETER FIRMIN

The Old Tree Stories

Foolish Miss Crow

A YOUNG YEARLING BOOK

Published by
Dell Publishing
a division of
Bantam Doubleday Dell Publishing Group, Inc.
666 Fifth Avenue
New York, New York 10103

This work was first published in Great Britain by Belitha Press Ltd.

ISBN: 0-440-40332-4

Reprinted by arrangement with Delacorte Press

Printed in the United States of America

September 1990

10 9 8 7 6 5 4 3 2 1

W

The Old Tree Stories

Miss Crow sat on a branch in the Old Tree.
"What a fine bird," said Mr Fox.
He took her picture with his camera.
Snip! Snap! Gotcha!!
"I could take a better picture if you
came a little closer," said cunning Mr Fox.

"Thank you, but no,"
said Miss Crow.

"Here's a pretty scarf for you to wear," said Mr Fox. "Come down and try it on."

"Oh, no!" said Miss Crow and she flew out of reach.

But Mr Fox left the scarf on a branch just in case she changed her mind.

And she DID.
She flew down to have a closer look.
"I'll just try it on,"
said Miss Crow.

Mr Fox took her picture with his camera.
Click! Snap! Gotcha!!
"Such a pretty Miss Crow," he said.

"Here's a beautiful hat," said Mr Fox. "Come just a little closer and we'll see if it fits."

"I said NO!" said Miss Crow,
and she flapped out of reach.
But he left it on a branch just
in case she changed her mind.

And she DID!
Miss Crow flew down
and tried on the hat.
"Mmm! Rather nice," she said.

Mr Fox took her picture with his camera.
Click! Snap! Gotcha!!

"I think you'd like this necklace," said Mr Fox. "Why not come a little closer and try it on for size?"

"My answer is still NO!" said Miss
Crow, and she struggled out of reach.
But he hung it on a branch
just in case she changed her mind.

AND SHE DID!
She flew down and put on the necklace.
She saw herself in the water.
"What a beautiful bird I am," she said.

Mr Fox took her picture with his camera.
Click! Snap! Gotcha!!
"Such a delicious Miss Crow," he said,
as he pounced!

"HELP!" squawked Miss Crow.
flapping her wings to get away.

But she was much too heavy to fly.
With the hat and the scarf and the
big sparkling jewels, she couldn't
get off the ground.
SNIP! SNAP! GOTCHA!!

So Mr Fox took her home for supper.